Hurricane!

By Patricia Lakin

illustrated by Vanessa Lubach

The Millbrook Press
Brookfield, Connecticut

For my mother, Eva Koretsky Lakin, who kept me safe during many a Cape Cod hurricane.

P.L.

For my niece, Kate Brown.

V.L.

Library of Congress Cataloging-in-Publication Data
Lakin, Pat.
Hurricane! / by Patricia Lakin ; illustrated by Vanessa Lubach.
p.   cm.
Summary: A girl and her father prepare their beach cottage for the coming hurricane, which topples their swing tree and washes away their stairs. Includes section of hurricane facts.
ISBN 0-7613-1616-7 (lib. bdg.)
[1. Hurricanes—Fiction. 2. Fathers and daughters—Fiction.] I. Lubach, Vanessa, ill. II. Title.
PZ7.L1586 Hu 2000   [E]—dc21   99-054839

Published by The Millbrook Press, Inc.
2 Old New Milford Road
Brookfield, Connecticut 06804
www.millbrookpress.com

My daddy and I spend every August in the cottage high on the bluff.

I can't wait to build sand castles and swim like a seal.

But first we unpack, then we set everything up.

We move the picnic table under the tree.

Daddy hangs my swing from a branch.

Then he gives me a push.

"I love it here," I say.

Then, like always, we run down the stairs to the beach and dive into the cool, calm water of the bay.

A few days later the waves come.

We've never had waves like this at our beach.

That afternoon, the radio gives us the news: A hurricane is heading our way.

It's called Hurricane Bob.

"What should we do?" I ask Daddy.

"Get ready," he said. "Tomorrow we'll have to put away or tie down everything outside."

"Why?"

"Because the hurricane's winds might blow them right away."

First thing in the morning, I race outside to
see what's happening.

Nothing!

Things look gray.

No seagulls squawk.

There's an eerie silence everywhere.

Nothing moves.

But we sure do!

We take down my swing, lash the picnic table to the tree, pack
up the garden chairs, and put away the barbecue. We put tape
on all the windowpanes to keep the wind from shattering them.

Rain begins to fall as we walk down to Mr. Finney's place.

The wind picks up as we help drag his rowboat up behind the dunes, close to his house.

"The hurricane is due to hit at 3 o'clock," says Daddy, looking at his watch. "We have just enough time to get some things in town."

It looks like the whole town is inside the supermarket.

One lady shoves me aside to grab candles from a shelf. Carts are piled high with stuff. The cashier's line is a mile long. Daddy and I get candles, batteries, and lots of tomato soup, plus my favorite treat: chocolate-covered raisins!

The wind shakes our car as we drive home.

Traffic lights swing back and forth. Street signs rattle. Rain pounds on the roof.

Mr. Finney is driving away from his house. He honks and waves good-bye.

"Where is he going?" I ask.

"The town opened up the school for people whose homes are close to the beach," said Daddy. "They'll be safer there."

"But our cottage is at the beach," I say.

"The waves won't come as high as the bluff. Our cottage will be as safe as the school."

When we get home, I open the car door. The wind almost blows it right off.

Daddy grabs my hand.

Rain cuts into our faces as we run to the front door.

Daddy turns on the radio. I turn on the lights.

I eat my chocolate-covered raisins and watch through the window.

The rain looks like razor-sharp teeth. The ocean is angry and dark. The waves have grown huge. They crash down onto the beach. Some take big bites from the dunes. The town dock looks like it's drowning. The boats are bobbing like toys in a tub. The wind wails through the walls of our house.

The lights flicker. Then they go out.

Daddy lights a candle.

I hear glass shatter. But I don't know what broke.

Then—C R A C K !

It's a branch from our tree.

It hangs down like a giant's broken arm.

"I'm scared," I tell Daddy. He holds me close.

"Try not to worry," Daddy tells me. "This house has stood through many a hurricane."

In a while, the rain
and the wind just stop.
The sun peeks out from a cloud.

"It's over!" I cheer.

"Only half over," Daddy says. "We're in the eye of the storm. Things
will be calm for a while. But the weather can get wilder than before."

Daddy's right!

The wind and the rain start all over again. But now the wind blows the
opposite way. Trees bend in half just like they were sticks.

"The wind's going to take us away!"

Daddy gets me a blanket. We watch lightning light up the sky.

CRACK—CRASH BAAM!

I rush back to the window.

"My swing tree!" I cry.

The roots are ripped right out of the ground.

"I hate hurricanes," I say.

"I know," says Daddy. "Mother Nature can do powerful things."

Then I see a wave break over Mr. Finney's house.

Slowly, the house splits in two. Then, silently, it slips into the sea, like the sand castles I build at the beach.

I put the blanket over my head. I can't watch this anymore.

Daddy's got the radio up to his ear. "They say the storm has almost passed."

By the time it's over, night has come.

It's too late to see all the damage that's been done.

It's black inside and out when it's time for bed. Daddy blows out the candles and kisses me goodnight.

The next morning we wake to a sky that's bright blue.

The ocean looks friendly and calm.

But nothing else looks the same.

Boats are scattered over the roads and lawns.

They look like schools of dead fish.

The beach is only a small sandy strip.

Half the parking lot has
been washed away.

Leaves and branches cover
the ground.

Trees have crashed everywhere.

We lost our swing tree and our stairs to the beach, but Mr. Finney
lost his whole house.

Electricity is out all over town.

Daddy says we won't have lights or TV for a week.

People everywhere are busy cleaning up.

The sound of buzz saws fills the air.

We cut up our tree to make firewood.

Mr. Finney tells us he'll rebuild his house.

He helps us build a new set of stairs.

The three of us see a helicopter whirr overhead.

It shoots down long lines with hooks on the ends.

People attach the hooks to a big sailboat.

The helicopter lifts the boat from a lawn.

Then the boat sails through the air.

We cheer when the boat floats again in the sea.

The next day Daddy and I plant a new tree.

"When can I hang my swing on its branch?"

"When you come back to this cottage with children of your own,"
Daddy says as he gives me a hug.

hurricane facts

What is a hurricane?
A hurricane is a tropical storm with winds that swirl around its center at speeds of at least 74 miles (118 kilometers) per hour.

Where do hurricanes form?
They form in most tropical oceans. Hurricanes that reach the eastern United States form in the Atlantic Ocean, off the coast of western Africa, just north of the equator.

What time of year is hurricane season?
In the eastern United States, hurricane season begins in the Northern Hemisphere's warm months—starting in June and lasting until October or even as late as November.

How does a hurricane move?
Hurricanes move in several ways:
- The actual storm swirls around and around in a counter-clockwise motion.
- The whole storm may then move west, across the Atlantic.
- Depending on other weather conditions, the hurricane may then move in a northerly direction.

How fast does a hurricane move?
Hurricanes can move over the sea as slowly as 10 miles (16 kilometers) an hour or as fast as 50 or 60 miles (80 or 96 kilometers) an hour.

What does a hurricane need to keep it powerful?
A hurricane needs warm ocean waters to keep its storm clouds filled with water vapor. A hurricane can lose speed and strength if it travels over cold water or moves over land areas. Most hurricanes die out at sea.

What does a hurricane look like?
Think of a hurricane as a huge swirling doughnut. Like the doughnut, there is a hole in its middle. This hole is called the hurricane's "eye."

What is the "eye" of the hurricane like?
There is little or no wind in the eye. A person may be able to see blue skies and even the sun shining through the hurricane's eye. Surrounding the eye is the eye wall. This is the part of the hurricane where the winds move the fastest.

How big is a hurricane?
Hurricanes can be about 10 miles high and hundreds of miles across. In 1999, Hurricane Floyd was unusually large at 700 miles (1,126 kilometers) wide. That is about the size of Texas.

Why are hurricanes so dangerous?
Sudden heavy rainfall, which causes flooding, and strong winds make hurricanes the most dangerous of storms. The worst coastal damage is caused by a hurricane's storm surge.

What is a storm surge?
A storm surge is like a wall or dome of water that the hurricane pushes along underneath it. Storm surges have caused ocean waters to rise as much as 25 to 30 feet (8 to 9 meters) above normal at the coast. That is as high as a three-story building.

Why is the storm surge so dangerous?
If a hurricane comes near land, the storm surge crashes onto shore, pushing everything out of its way and causing great flooding.

What can be done to stop a hurricane?

Nothing! But knowing where, when, how, and with what force the storm will strike helps people prepare for the storm. If people know what to expect, they can lessen some of a hurricane's damage. And, more importantly, being prepared can save lives.

How can people know if a hurricane is coming?

Newspaper, radio, and television reports give people the latest information about a hurricane's strength and probable path. But weather experts admit that they can't always predict the path of a storm.

How can people prepare for the storm?

- Tie down any loose outdoor objects or bring them indoors.
- Tape up or cover windows with plywood to keep large pieces of glass from shattering.
- Stock up on candles, batteries, bottled water, and types of food that don't need to be cooked.

How can people stay safe in a hurricane?

People should follow the instructions given by their town officials. That may mean evacuating, or leaving, their homes to go to a safer building that is farther inland.

Why do hurricanes have names?

During hurricane season, there could be more than one storm that threatens an area. The naming of storms helps scientists and people tell each storm apart.

How long have hurricanes been named?

This practice began in 1953. At first only female names were used. Male names were added in 1979. The names of very destructive storms are retired, never to be used again.

Do hurricanes occur in other parts of the world?

Yes, but they are not known as hurricanes. They are called typhoons in the China Sea and cyclones in the Indian Ocean.

How did this fiercest of storms get its name?

Some people think the "hurricane" was named after *Hunraken*, storm god of the ancient Central American Mayan people. Others say it was named for *Huracán*, the Caribbean native people's god of stormy weather.

Do hurricanes do any good?

Like all forces of nature, along with the damage they cause, hurricanes can help balance elements in nature by bringing large amounts of rainfall to areas that may need it.